FRIENDS
OF ACPL

Elaine and the Flying Frog

Written and Illustrated by
Heidi Chang

Previously titled *Elaine, Mary Lewis, and the Frogs*

A STEPPING STONE BOOK

Random House 🏠 New York

Copyright © 1988 by Heidi Chang
All rights reserved under International and Pan-American Copyright Conventions. Published in the United States by Random House, Inc., New York. Originally published by Crown Publishers, Inc., in 1988 as *Elaine, Mary Lewis, and the Frogs.*

Library of Congress Cataloging-in-Publication Data
Chang, Heidi. [Elaine, Mary Lewis, and the frogs] Elaine and the flying frog / story and illustrations by Heidi Chang. p. cm. (A Stepping Stone book) Original title: Elaine, Mary Lewis, and the frogs. Summary: Chinese American Elaine Chow feels like an outcast after moving to a small town in Iowa, until she shares a new friendship and a science project with a girl strongly interested in frogs. ISBN 0-679-80870-1 (trade) : ISBN 0-679-90870-6 (lib. bdg.) : [1. Chinese Americans—Fiction. 2. Friendship—Fiction. 3. Iowa—Fiction. 4. Frogs—Fiction.] I. Title. [PZ7.C359664E1 1991] [Fic]—dc20 90-33721 CIP AC

Manufactured in the United States of America 1 2 3 4 5 6 7 8 9 10

To my mother and late father,
who left their homeland so many years ago

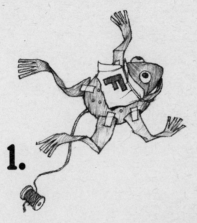

1.

Elaine Chow was on her way to her first day in her new school. As she walked, she thought about how much she missed playing jump rope with her old friends on the hilly streets in San Francisco. This Iowa land was so flat! Elaine put her hand inside her coat pocket and felt for her jump rope. She always carried it for good luck. She had a feeling she would be needing good luck today.

Inside Eleanor Roosevelt Elementary

School all the kids seemed to know where they were going.

Elaine decided to ask an older girl for help. "Excuse me," she said. "Can you help me find room 312?"

"Sure. I'm going upstairs too," the girl said. "Who's your teacher?"

"Ms. Bonovox, it says." Elaine showed the girl her registration card.

"Ms. Bonovox!" the girl exclaimed. "I had her last year."

"You did?" Elaine said. "What's she like?

I came to school last week to meet the principal, but I didn't get to meet my teacher."

"Oh, she's okay. She's just different." The girl stopped. "Here's your room. Good luck!"

Elaine smiled at the girl and then turned to go into her classroom. There at the door was the teacher, greeting each student who came into the room. She did look different. She was dressed completely in black. She had big black sunglasses dangling from a long black cord around her neck. The patterns on her stockings reminded Elaine of Japanese rice crackers, with their star and triangle shapes.

Elaine handed the teacher her registration card. "Hello, Elaine," the woman said. "I'm Ms. Bonovox. Let's see, it says here you used to live in San Francisco. I used to live there too."

Elaine was excited. "You're from San Francisco?"

"Well, no. I was born and raised in New York City. But I lived in San Francisco for a few years. Some days I really miss the sea

air and pink houses. But you know, Elaine,
I like it here. I hope you do too."

I hope so, Elaine thought.

"Children, please find your desks now,"
said Ms. Bonovox. Elaine quickly took a seat
in the first row. A girl stood in front of her.

"You're sitting at my desk," the girl said. Elaine was startled. "What?" she said.

"See, the names are always on the desks the first day of school. That's so we know where to sit. This desk says *Kelleen Burke.* That's me." She stared at Elaine. "You must be new here."

"Oh, I'm sorry," Elaine said. Then she felt silly. It sounded as if she were sorry for being new! She looked around the room and quickly found her desk. It was right behind Kelleen's.

Elaine could smell the wax on her new desk. She remembered the desk she had had in her old school. She had carved her initials in it before she left for Iowa. Her friends Jeffrey, Kimiko, and Sherry had, too. "We'll always be friends," Elaine had said to them bravely. But now she didn't feel at all brave.

Ms. Bonovox's voice cut into Elaine's thoughts. "Class, this morning we are going to have our pictures taken for the bulletin board." Ms. Bonovox was holding a camera— the kind that prints pictures instantly. "I've cut out fall leaves and written your names on them to put beneath your pictures. That way we can all get to know each other."

After Ms. Bonovox took their pictures, she handed out white paper, colored pencils, and crayons.

"I want you to draw something," Ms. Bonovox said. "Draw the most exciting thing you did this summer."

Elaine was happy. She had her own crayons at home—the largest set you could buy. It even came with a built-in sharpener. Now she started a picture of her moving day. First she drew a huge truck with *Mayflower* written on the side. It stood on a big hill. Then she put herself and her cat, Mei Lee, in the picture. They stood next to their old house waving good-bye to Pau-Pah, Elaine's grandmother.

Elaine worked hard at her drawing. She didn't notice the teacher looking over her shoulder until Ms. Bonovox said, "That's very good, Elaine." Elaine felt proud.

Kelleen turned around and wrinkled her

nose at Elaine in a funny way. Elaine smiled back. But Kelleen quickly faced front again and then leaned over to look at the paper of the boy next to her.

For a minute Elaine got an odd feeling in her stomach. Then she saw Ms. Bonovox smile at her. It was more like half a smile, but something about it was special—it was just as if Ms. Bonovox knew what Elaine was feeling. Elaine looked down at her drawing again and let out a deep sigh.

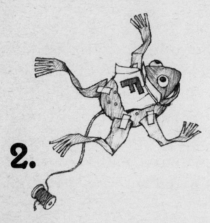

2.

By the time the bell rang for lunch Elaine was almost dizzy. It was partly because so much new was happening and partly because she was starving. She couldn't wait to eat. Her mother had made fried rice. Since it was her first day of school, Mrs. Chow had even chopped up pieces of barbecued pork into it.

Elaine took her lunchbox out of her desk and walked down to the lunchroom with the rest of the class. As she stood looking around for a place to sit, a boy ran into her with a tray. Two girls in front of Elaine were trying to see who could eat the fastest. Elaine sat down at the other end of the table. She unsnapped the fasteners on her tin lunch container.

"What's that?" It was Kelleen. She was peering down at Elaine's lunchbox.

Now Kelleen sat down. "Is that your *lunch*box? It looks like it's for carrying pencils!"

Kelleen's lunchbox was bright pink plastic with kids on it who had strawberries for heads. Elaine opened her metal lunchbox.

"What's that you're eating?" Kelleen went on. "It looks like rice with little colored squares and circles."

"It *is* rice. It's fried rice with peas, carrots, and little pieces of pork in it," Elaine said. Hadn't Kelleen ever seen fried rice before?

Kelleen held out her sandwich. It was baloney. "How come you don't have a sandwich?"

"I always have rice for lunch," Elaine answered. "Do you always have baloney sandwiches for lunch?"

"No, sometimes I have tuna, or peanut butter if my mother forgets to go to the grocery store. I'd get tired of eating baloney every day. Don't you get tired of eating rice all the time?"

"No," said Elaine. "I like rice. I have it for breakfast and dinner too. In the morning I get rice porridge with a lot of good leftovers mixed in." Elaine smiled, but Kelleen was making a face at Elaine's rice.

"Wow, I can't imagine having rice for breakfast. I usually have cereal. I like Sundays best, though, because then we have pancakes after church. Hey!" Kelleen said suddenly. "I'll give you some of my baloney sandwich if you want."

"That's okay," said Elaine. "If you're tired of baloney, do you want some of my fried rice?"

"No, thank you," Kelleen said in an oddly polite way, as if she were answering a grownup. "I think I'll trade it. There's Harry. I bet *he'll* trade. Harry!" she called, and ran off.

Elaine looked into her lunchbox. She didn't feel hungry anymore. She wished she had something to trade. She hadn't even had a chance to ask Kelleen if she liked to jump rope.

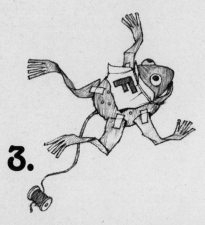

3.

The next morning, when Elaine sat down for her breakfast of rice, she stared at her bowl of *jook*—steaming rice porridge—for a long time.

"What's wrong, Elaine?" her mother asked. "You were so quiet yesterday after your first day of school. You are quiet now, too. That's not like you."

"Mom, why do we eat rice for breakfast instead of cereal like they do here? This one girl in class acted like she never saw anyone eating rice before!"

"We've been eating rice for years, Elaine. It didn't start with you. I ate rice growing up, and so did my mother. But you can have cereal if you like instead."

Elaine just finished her rice porridge.

As she walked to school, Elaine saw a few familiar faces. She smiled at some girls and boys. It seemed as if they didn't even see her. Maybe they thought she was strange, walking all by herself and smiling. The smile froze on her face and she got a lump in her throat. It felt like the time she had gotten butterscotch candy stuck there and couldn't breathe. Or like the time her parents told her they were moving to Iowa.

She remembered that day. Her mother and father had called her into the living room.

"Elaine, your father and I have something to tell you," said Elaine's mother.

Right away, Elaine thought something bad had happened. Maybe her cat had run away from home. "Did Mei Lee run away?" she asked.

"No, Elaine," Mr. Chow said. He gave his daughter a hug. "It's nothing like that. It's—we are going to move."

"Move? Where? In with Pau-Pah?" Elaine asked. Pau-Pah, Elaine's grandmother, lived down the block.

"No. We are moving far away," Mr. Chow said.

"How far? As far as cousin Hwai-Hwai

lives, across the ocean? Are we going to take an airplane?"

"Well, not as far as China, but we will have to take an airplane. We are moving to a place called Cedarville, Iowa. I'm going to do work for a university near there."

"What kind of work? Can't you just do it here and mail it to them?"

"That would be nice, but I have to be there to help them with a big project. They need me to tell them what to do. Just the way you need your teacher at school."

So Elaine had had to leave all her friends and Pau-Pah, too. At least Mei Lee got to move with them. Still it was awfully hard not to have anyone but Mei Lee to talk to. "Jeffrey and Kimiko, do you miss me like I miss you?" she said half out loud.

In class Ms. Bonovox announced, "We are going to begin a science project. We will study flying objects. You will all have a partner. Today we will go on a field trip to look at butterflies."

Elaine's partner was Mary Lewis Thorp. Elaine knew her name. When the Chow family moved to Cedarville, Mary Lewis's mother had brought a huge basket of fruit to the Chow family to welcome them. She was nice.

"Hi," Mary Lewis said, coming up to Elaine. "My name is Mary Lewis. Do you like butterflies?"

"Yes, but I don't like to catch them," Elaine said.

"Me neither. I would rather catch frogs down at the creek. I wish they could fly. Then maybe we could study frogs instead of butterflies."

"I've never seen a real frog," Elaine said. "Only in my science books."

"You haven't?" Mary Lewis said. "Well, maybe we can sneak off later and I'll show you a real one!"

But Ms. Bonovox had strict rules. She made everyone stay in a group on the field trip.

"Ms. Bonovox sure watches us like a hawk," Mary Lewis complained. "How does she do it? She's always wearing those dark sunglasses."

Elaine liked Ms. Bonovox. "Maybe she can't see without them," she said.

"I think she wears them so they'll match

her black outfits," said Mary Lewis. "I'm surprised she doesn't make us catch only black butterflies." She giggled.

"Oh, I like that one with the yellow wing tips!" Elaine said. She ran after it.

"Now, remember," Ms. Bonovox said when they got back to the classroom, "we are to let these go after class. So don't even think about putting them into a photo album or sticking them onto pins. We are only going to observe how they fly. Did you know that butterflies' wings are a lot like birds' wings? Dragonflies and ordinary houseflies move their wings much faster. The rapid motion causes the buzzing sound you hear."

"I think butterflies are a lot prettier than flies," said Kelleen. "I don't even know why we have flies. My cat, Mork, eats them all the time. Why do we have flies, Ms. Bonovox?"

"One time my cat ate a fly and threw up on my mom!" Harry said.

"Harry, you're so gross!" Mary Lewis said, making a face.

Elaine thought, *He's sort of cute.* If she turned her head to one side, he looked a little like Jeffrey. Well, just a bit. She started to laugh at Harry, but the rest of the class was groaning.

"I think we have flies so frogs can eat them," Mary Lewis said.

"You've asked a good question, Kelleen," said Ms. Bonovox. "Class, I would like you to look that up in your science book tonight for homework." Everyone groaned again.

"Thanks a lot, Kelleen," Mary Lewis said.

"And for Monday I want you and your partner to bring in a flying object. I'll give you these few days and the weekend to think of something," Ms. Bonovox added.

"From nature, or man-made?" asked Harry.

"Either one. Be creative!"

"And don't you dare bring in anything disgusting or I'll scream," Kelleen said to Harry.

Mary Lewis waved her hand in the air. "How about a frog, Ms. Bonovox?" she asked.

"Mary Lewis, honestly, do frogs fly?" asked Ms. Bonovox.

"Well, no," Mary Lewis said.

"It seems you've answered your own question," the teacher said.

"I wonder if there *is* a way to make frogs fly," Mary Lewis whispered to Elaine. "Do you want to go down to the creek after school? I'll show you plenty of frogs."

"Oh, yes," Elaine said.

"Mary Lewis and Elaine, please save your whispers until class is over," Ms. Bonovox said. She peered at them over her glasses.

Elaine had to struggle to keep from talking to Mary Lewis for the rest of the day. She couldn't wait to see a creek filled with frogs.

Elaine remembered what her grandmother had told her about making friends. "Friends are like flowers, Elaine." She and Elaine were planting bok choy—Chinese cabbage—in the garden. "You must be patient with them. It takes time for beautiful things to grow."

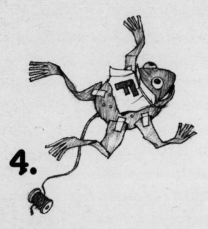

4.

Finally school was over. Elaine and Mary Lewis set out for the creek. "Mary Lewis," Elaine asked, "how come you have two first names?"

"I was named after my great-great-great-aunt. She came here a long time ago from down South. Virginia, I think. I have another aunt named Mary Lewis, too. My family likes handing down that name for some reason." Mary Lewis shrugged. "It *is* kind of different, isn't it? I guess I'm kind of an oddball around here."

"My name is different, too," said Elaine.

"*Elaine*'s not different," said Mary Lewis.

"Well, Elaine is only my English name. My parents named me that because it's the closest they could get to my Chinese name."

"Your Chinese name? What's that?" Mary Lewis asked.

Elaine hesitated for a moment. Then she answered, "Oi Lai. Well, I guess it's not close."

"Oi Lai, Oi Lai," Mary Lewis repeated. For an instant Elaine thought Mary Lewis might make a face the way Kelleen had when she saw the fried rice. But instead Mary Lewis asked, "Are you named after someone, the way I am?"

"No, not really. When my mother was my age she lived in the mountains of China. Every day on her way to school she passed these flowers near her home. They were yellow orchids. When she came to America she missed them so much she decided to name me after them. So my name really means *orchid*."

"Gosh, I wish I could be named after something I like," Mary Lewis said. "But I suppose I couldn't go around with a name like Frog Thorp."

Elaine laughed. She thought Mary Lewis was really funny.

"Oh, look there, Elaine! I think I see a frog!" Mary Lewis shouted. She ran down to the edge of the creek.

Elaine followed. It was a long, winding creek with high weeds and cattails growing everywhere. It smelled funny, too. As Elaine watched, Mary Lewis scooped a frog up into her hands. Elaine jumped back.

"Don't be scared," Mary Lewis said. She held out the struggling frog.

Elaine stuck out a finger to feel its skin. The frog blinked its eyes at her.

"They've got really sticky tongues," Mary Lewis said. "Sometimes I pretend I'm a frog when I eat my cereal. But I have to do it when my mother's not looking. She says it isn't good table manners."

Elaine laughed. "I would like to try that sometime!"

"It works best with Froot Loops or Cheerios," Mary Lewis said, rolling her tongue out and back like a frog.

"How about rice?"

"Sure, rice sticks to your tongue too," Mary Lewis said.

Elaine smiled and tried rolling her tongue. She was glad Mary Lewis hadn't asked her all kinds of questions about eating rice.

"Did you know some people eat frogs?" Mary Lewis asked. She set the frog on a rock. It scrambled away into the water.

"I eat fish," Elaine said. "But I don't think I could eat a frog."

"Me neither!"

Then Mary Lewis showed Elaine how to skip rocks across the creek. "Watch this," she said, rubbing a flat rock on her skirt. She bent down low and flipped the rock into the creek. The rock skipped twice over the water.

"Do you want to try?" she asked. "You have to use a really flat rock." She handed

Elaine a rock from the edge of the creek.

Elaine flung it out into the water, but it just sank.

"You have to flip it out of your hand, like this." Mary Lewis took a rock and showed Elaine.

"Like this?" Elaine picked up another flat rock and tried again. This time her rock skimmed across the water.

"Yeah, you did it!" yelled Mary Lewis.

Elaine couldn't stop smiling. It felt like the time she first learned to blow a bubble with her gum. It took a whole week, but when Elaine could finally blow a bubble, she couldn't stop. Elaine didn't want to stop skipping rocks, either. Pretty soon Mary Lewis and Elaine had skipped practically every flat rock they could find.

"Gosh, Elaine, I wish there was some way we could make a frog fly," said Mary Lewis as they started for home.

"Yeah. They turn into frogs from tadpoles. Too bad they can't become butterflies after that," Elaine said.

"Too bad we can't live in Disneyland either," said Mary Lewis.

"Well, I'll try really hard to think of a project tonight," Elaine said.

"Me too," said Mary Lewis.

Elaine couldn't wait to go home and tell her mother all about her new friend. Soon she was running.

"Mom, Mom," Elaine said, charging into the house. Her mother was breaking string beans at the kitchen table.

"Mom, I met this girl at school today," Elaine said. "She's real nice and taught me all about frogs."

"Slow down, Elaine," Mrs. Chow said. "Why don't you sit down? Do you want some water?"

"No, thanks," Elaine said, sitting down at the table. She wondered why everybody always thought you needed water when you got excited.

"What's her name?"

"Mary Lewis. She's the daughter of that Mrs. Thorp who came over with the fruit."

Elaine started to eat the string beans out of the strainer.

"Elaine, stop it. We're going to have supper soon." Mrs. Chow moved the strainer out of Elaine's reach. *"Eiyah!"* she exclaimed. "Where have you been in your shoes?"

Elaine looked at her shoes. She had forgotten to take them off before coming into the house. "We went down to the creek to look at frogs," Elaine said. Her mother frowned. It was a rule to take your shoes off when you came inside.

"I think I'll go play now," Elaine said, getting up from the table.

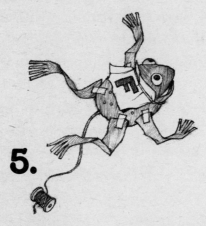

5.

Elaine hurried into the den. She took the pillows off the couch and lined them up in a row on the floor. Then she crouched very low and jumped as high as she could, flinging out her arms and legs. She was jumping like a frog! She pounced down on the big pillows one after another, barely missing Mei Lee's tail. Mei Lee had a lot of fun darting back and forth around Elaine and the pillows.

Mrs. Chow came into the den. "Elaine,

look what you've done to this room!" she cried.

"I'm a frog, Mother!" Elaine said. She took another big leap and fell down onto the pillows.

"Tell me, Elaine, who did you like meeting better? Mary Lewis or the frogs?" Mrs. Chow asked, picking up a pillow each time Elaine jumped to another one. "And

you still have your shoes on! *Eiyah!* Go outside and jump where real frogs jump, Elaine. I don't want you to hit your head on the furniture like cousin Hwai-Hwai did when you were both jumping off the couch."

"Oh, Mom. We were just little kids then. We were airplanes!"

"So she cracked her head open for being an airplane," Mrs. Chow said.

Elaine started buzzing around like a jet.

"I don't understand you sometimes, Elaine. Now go outside until suppertime." Mrs. Chow pointed toward the door.

At the supper table Elaine tried to sneak in some practice rolling her tongue in and out with rice on it.

"Elaine, what are you doing?" Mr. Chow asked.

Elaine looked up from her rice bowl with her tongue still curled. But she couldn't really talk like that. She uncurled her tongue and answered, "Eating like a frog."

"What?" Mr. Chow said.

"Oh, Elaine met a girl in school today who's crazy about frogs. It's that nice Mrs. Thorp's daughter. Apparently she's been teaching Elaine all about frogs."

"Her name is Mary Lewis, Daddy," said Elaine.

"Do Mary Lewis's parents let her make those faces at the dinner table?" Mr. Chow asked.

"No, she only does it when her mother's not looking."

"All I can say is she must be awfully skinny. You will be, too, Elaine, if you don't eat your food properly. Sit up straight."

"I was just trying to see how frogs eat, Daddy. Besides, I would rather have rice any day over flies and gnats."

"Elaine, I don't think this is table conversation," her mother said.

"What else did you learn in school today besides eating like a frog?" Mr. Chow asked.

"Well, Ms. Bonovox—that's my teacher," Elaine said, "has us studying flying objects in science class."

"Isn't she the teacher we saw who wears those dark glasses?" Mr. Chow asked.

"She told me she used to live in San Francisco!"

"Really?" Mr. Chow said.

"Yes, that's right. Mrs. Thorp mentioned her," said Mrs. Chow. "She's supposed to be some sort of artist. Everyone seems to think she's very creative with the children."

"Do you like Ms. Bonovox, Elaine?" asked Mr. Chow.

"I do. Some of the kids think she's weird. But she's not! She's just—different. Ms. Bonovox wants us to bring in a flying object next week for our project in class."

"What sort of flying object?" Elaine's father asked.

"Well, Mary Lewis wanted to bring in a frog. But frogs don't fly. Can you help me think of a project?"

"Why don't you come down to my workshop after supper? Perhaps we can think something up together," Mr. Chow said.

Mr. Chow's workshop was in the basement. He liked to build things. Most of all he loved to build kites.

When Mr. Chow went down to his workshop after supper, Elaine was already there. She was jumping all over the basement.

"Elaine, what are you doing now?" her father asked.

Elaine stumbled into the worktable and upset a bottle of glue. It fell on the floor.

"Sorry, Daddy," she said, and picked it up.

"Come here, Elaine. I think I have an idea for this flying project of yours."

"You do?" Elaine said. "What?"

"Well, since you are so interested in frogs, why not make a frog into a kite? That way you could bring in a frog and also an object that flies."

"Daddy! That's the best idea for a flying object I ever heard!" Elaine said, beaming. "But can you help us? I don't think Mary Lewis knows how to build a kite. And *I* don't."

"I would be delighted to help build this best idea for a flying object," said Mr. Chow. And he gave his daughter a big hug.

The next morning Elaine ran almost all the way to school. She saw her friend on the playground. "Mary Lewis! Mary Lewis!" she called, running across the grass.

"Hi, Elaine," Mary Lewis greeted her. "I tried all last night to think of something good for our school project. But I couldn't."

Just then Kelleen walked up. "Hi," she

said. "What are you guys bringing in next week for science?"

"We don't know yet," Mary Lewis said. Kelleen seemed to be waiting for them to ask her something.

"Well, in case you wanted to know, I'm bringing in a ladybug," Kelleen told them.

"Oh, that's nice," Elaine said.

"Yeah, well, I thought so too." Kelleen smiled. "I suppose you still want to bring in a frog, Mary Lewis. Silly. Frogs can't fly."

Elaine could tell that Mary Lewis was trying awfully hard not to push Kelleen down or call her Stinky Pinky, Mary Lewis's secret nickname for her.

"Oh, there's Melinda Pappajohn," Kelleen said. "I heard she was bringing in a bat! I should go tell her about my ladybug."

"Boy, she makes me so mad sometimes," Mary Lewis said after Kelleen left. "I almost called her Stinky Pinky to her face!"

"Never mind her, Mary Lewis. Listen, I have an idea," Elaine said.

"What?"

"Why *not* make a frog fly?"

"Just how are we supposed to do that? Put a zillion fly wings on it?"

"Gross! No, we can't make a real frog fly, but we can make a frog into a kite," Elaine explained.

Mary Lewis frowned. "I don't know how to make a kite. Do you?"

"Well, just a little bit I do. But that doesn't matter. My father is going to help us. He builds kites as a hobby. He can even make one out of bamboo and rice paper."

"Gee, where are we going to get stuff like that to build a kite?"

"My dad already has it. You'll see."

"Really?" Mary Lewis said, her eyes widening.

"Really. Why don't you come over to my house on Saturday? My father can help us then."

"Wow, a frog that flies!" Mary Lewis grinned. "Won't Ms. Bonovox be surprised."

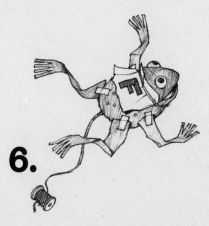

6.

Mary Lewis rode up the Chows' driveway at nine o'clock Saturday morning. Her green bike had a frog's-head horn on the handlebars.

Elaine dashed out to the porch to greet her. "Hi, Mary Lewis!" she called, waving.

Elaine's mother came out of the house too. "You must be Mary Lewis. Elaine hasn't stopped talking about you. She jumped all over the den pretending to be a frog."

"Well, frogs are cool, Mrs. Chow," said

Mary Lewis. "I hope someday to have my own frog farm. I'm going to call it the Mary Lewis Frog Farm."

"Sounds like a good name to me." Mrs. Chow smiled. "Would you girls like something to drink? How about some juice?"

"What's that you're drinking?" Mary Lewis asked, peering into Mrs. Chow's cup.

"Tea."

"I always thought tea came in little bags. What are those floating things?"

"They're tea leaves, Mary Lewis." Mrs. Chow laughed. "Tea can also come like this. These leaves are grown in my hometown in China and then are shipped here. Come with me. I'll show you how I use them."

Mrs. Chow put some water to boil on the stove. Then she spooned some tea leaves into a teapot.

"Mrs. Chow," Mary Lewis said as Elaine's mother poured the hot water into the teapot, "could I have tea instead of juice?"

"Of course you may, Mary Lewis." Mrs. Chow poured tea for both girls.

Mary Lewis watched as a few tea leaves swirled around in her cup.

"Looks like you've got a boyfriend," said Mrs. Chow.

"You mean that Sammy in the fourth grade? How do you know about him?"

Mrs. Chow laughed. "Whenever you get a stray tea leaf in your cup it means you have a boyfriend."

"Oh," Mary Lewis said. She blushed a little.

After they finished their tea, Elaine took

Mary Lewis by the arm and pulled her down the stairs.

"Come on, Mary Lewis. My dad is waiting for us."

Mary Lewis was amazed by all the kites hanging up in the Chows' basement. "Wow!

Did your father make all of these?" she asked.

"Well, some of them my grandfather built. He taught my father to make kites, and his father taught him."

"Gee, my mom's been trying to teach me how to knit, but I think learning how to build a kite is much more exciting. How long does it take to make one?"

"It depends on what kind of kite," Elaine said. "I suppose the same way it is with knitting."

"I hope not," Mary Lewis said, crossing her arms. "Do you know it's taken my mom almost a whole year to knit me a sweater?"

Elaine laughed.

"Hello there, girls," said Mr. Chow, looking up from his worktable. He was busily twisting string around some wooden strips. "So you want to make a flying frog?"

"Oh, yes," Mary Lewis said, walking over to the table. "It's so nice of you to help, Mr. Chow. I don't know how to make a kite."

"I'm happy to help, Mary Lewis. Building kites is something I regard very highly. Kites were invented in China, you know."

"They were?" said Mary Lewis.

"Yes, almost two thousand years ago," said Mr. Chow.

"Wow, that's older than my mother's tea set! The one Great-aunt Mary Lewis from Virginia gave her."

"Well, China's a very old country," said Mr. Chow.

"Tell how they invented kites, Dad," said Elaine.

"I always thought Benjamin Franklin invented the kite," Mary Lewis said.

"There are a lot of stories about how the kite helped Benjamin Franklin experiment with electricity. But originally kites were made for war," said Mr. Chow.

"Many years ago—even before your great-aunt Mary Lewis's tea set—a Chinese general used a kite to figure out how far away his enemy was. The wind carried the kite to the enemy fortress. The general pulled the kite back and measured the string. Then he knew just how long to make the tunnels that led up to the fortress. And his surprise attack won the war."

"Maybe the people who saw the kites were scared," said Mary Lewis.

"That's right," said Mr. Chow. "The villagers who saw the strange flying objects didn't know what they were. They called them magical spirits or messages from the gods."

"Yeah, except for the clever general and his soldiers!" Elaine said.

"Then kites became popular," said Mr. Chow. "And they were used for festivals, not battles. Kites in different shapes took on different meanings. Some kites were said to give good luck. Others were used to frighten evil spirits away. Crane kites and turtle kites meant long life."

"Did they ever use frogs, Mr. Chow?" Mary Lewis asked.

"I don't know. I think you girls will have to come up with your own meaning for a frog kite." Mr. Chow held up the wooden strips he had been tying together with string.

"Gosh! It really looks like a frog," Mary Lewis said.

"But what can *we* do, Dad?" Elaine asked.

"Yes, we have to help, or it won't be our project," Mary Lewis said.

"Okay. Why don't you take some of this rice paper and paint it green? Make it look like a frog's skin."

Elaine and Mary Lewis went to work painting the rice paper with watercolors. Elaine found some gold sequins, and they began pasting those all over the paper too.

"Elaine, what do you suppose a frog kite would mean?" Mary Lewis asked her. A gold sequin was stuck to her thumb, and she pulled it off.

"How are you two doing?" Mr. Chow asked. "Looks like you've gotten more sequins on yourselves than on the frog."

"It's hard, Daddy," said Elaine. "The glue dries too fast for us." She began picking sequins off her sweatshirt.

"Well, that's pretty good," Mr. Chow said, admiring the work Elaine and Mary Lewis had done on the rice paper. "I think we can put this paper on the frog's body now."

"We can?" Mary Lewis said. "How are we going to do that?"

"Carefully!" said Mr. Chow. He smiled. "It takes a lot of glue, and I wouldn't want to send you home all sticky like a candy apple, Mary Lewis."

The girls pasted the rice paper onto the frog's body and attached yellow streamers to its sides. They drew eyes on its face with black crayon and used two Ping-Pong balls for its eyeballs.

"I do think that's the best-looking kite in Iowa," said Mr. Chow. "Don't you agree?"

Elaine and Mary Lewis beamed.

"I can't wait to take it to school on Monday. Can we fly it yet?" Mary Lewis asked.

Mr. Chow shook his head. "It's still a bit wet. But I think by Monday it will be just fine."

"Fantastic!" Elaine said. "Won't Ms. Bonovox be pleased!"

"Ms. Bonovox—and me too!" said Mary Lewis.

7.

Early Monday morning Mary Lewis and Elaine carried the kite to school. They had put it in a plastic garbage bag to keep it a surprise.

They set the garbage bag on the project table and the whole class came around.

"What is it?" Harry asked. "I'll tell you what mine is if you tell me what yours is. I brought in a moth."

"Well, it's a—" began Elaine.

Mary Lewis nudged her.

Wing Lake Chow
May Chow, Elaine Chow
330 Meadow Crest

Mei Lee

"No, Harry, it's a surprise," she said. "You'll see."

"It looks like our Christmas tree stuck in a garbage bag after New Year's Day," Kelleen said.

Mary Lewis gave Kelleen a cold stare. Kelleen moved away from the table.

"Okay, class, that's enough. Please return to your seats," said Ms. Bonovox. "Who would like to go first with their science project?"

A few children raised their hands. Ms. Bonovox picked Harry.

"I caught this moth right outside my house," said Harry. He held up a jar with a gray moth fluttering in it. "It made a cocoon right on our tree in the front yard. There used to be a bunch of them, but my mom knocked them down."

"Why did she do that, Harry?" asked a boy who sat next to Elaine.

"She didn't want them flying into the house every time I opened the door. And she said they would eat my sweaters and socks. Would they do that, Ms. Bonovox? What happens when they go to the bathroom?"

The class began to laugh.

"Harry, that's enough for now," Ms. Bonovox said. Then she saw Mary Lewis's hand waving and sighed. "All right, Mary Lewis, you can be next. You've had your arm up and down so much you could lead us in gym class today."

"Oh, goody. Do you want to see a frog fly, Ms. Bonovox?"

"If it's possible."

"Hey, Ms. Bonovox, anything is possible!" said Mary Lewis.

The kids circled around the mystery in the garbage bag. Elaine and Mary Lewis slowly and carefully removed the covering from the kite. The sequins on its bright green body sparkled, and its Ping-Pong eyeballs jiggled as the two girls held it up. The class oohed and aahed.

"Hey," Kelleen said. "That doesn't look anything like an old Christmas tree. It looks like a kite. A *frog kite!*"

"Does it fly?" someone asked.

"Of course it does, silly," Mary Lewis said. "Elaine's father helped us build it. Did you know that kites came from China over two thousand years ago?"

"Hey, Mary Lewis, that's older than your great-aunt's tea set," said Harry.

"I know, and I used to think that was really old. Did you know kites have special meanings?"

"Elaine, can you tell us about that?" Ms. Bonovox asked.

"Well, a dragon kite means good fish-

ing," Elaine said. "And crane kites mean long life. So do turtle kites."

"What about a frog?" asked Harry.

"I think a frog means . . ." Mary Lewis looked at Elaine. "Friendship! Isn't that right, Elaine?"

"Oh, yes, a frog kite means friendship," Elaine said, smiling happily.

"How fascinating," said Ms. Bonovox. She was smiling too. "Class, wouldn't you agree?"

"Oh, yes!" the whole class chimed in together.

The bell rang for recess. Everybody ran to their cubbyholes to get their jackets. "Elaine, we were a big hit," Mary Lewis said.

"Yeah. I told my father it was the best idea for a flying object," said Elaine as she put on her jacket.

"You were right," Mary Lewis said. She reached into her cubbyhole for her jacket.

Suddenly Elaine noticed a rope on the top shelf of Mary Lewis's cubbyhole.

"Mary Lewis," she said, "is that a jump rope?"

"Sure," Mary Lewis said. She pulled it out to show Elaine.

"Gee, Mary Lewis, I didn't know you liked to jump rope," said Elaine. "Look. Sometimes I even carry my jump rope in my pocket for good luck." She pulled the rope out to show Mary Lewis.

"Wow!" said Mary Lewis. "You must *really* like to jump rope!"

"All the way to Mexico!" Elaine said.

"Hey, I know that one!" Mary Lewis laughed.

Elaine couldn't wait to get to the playground.

"How about, 'Teddy bear, teddy bear . . .' "

"Sitting in a golden chair!" chanted Mary Lewis.

"Thinks he is a millionaire!" they finished together.

"Hey, what are you guys doing?" Kelleen asked. She was sitting on the ground drawing a game of hopscotch on the sidewalk. Mary Lewis and Elaine had walked right into one of her neatly chalked pink squares.

"We're going to jump rope. Do you want to jump rope with us, Kelleen?" asked Elaine.

"I just got a new jump rope yesterday. It's pink. It matches my lunchbox. It's in my cubbyhole, though."

"Hey, Elaine," said Harry, walking over to them. "Would you like to go look for some worms?"

"Ugh," Mary Lewis said, making a face.

"Harry, are you going to be gross again?" asked Kelleen. "I'll scream. I swear I will."

"We're going to jump rope," Elaine said to Harry. "Want to join us?"

"That's for girls," Harry said.

"It is not," Mary Lewis said. "Don't you know boxers jump rope?"

"Sure I know that," said Harry quickly. He thought for a moment. "I'll just hold the end of the rope," he said.

"I'll hold the other end," said Kelleen.

"Okay," Elaine said. She and Mary Lewis tied their ropes together. Harry and Kelleen started swinging.

Mary Lewis jumped in first.

"I like coffee.

"I like tea . . ." she sang.

"I would like my friend Elaine . . . to
jump in with me!"

And Elaine jumped in.

About the Author and Illustrator

Heidi Chang has been drawing ever since she can remember. "Recently my mother found some drawings of mine from when I was two. And I've been drawing ever since. I also love to write, and sometimes I write about people I know."

When Heidi goes to visit her family in California, she loves to hang out and watch cartoons with her niece and nephews. "We also go hunting for dinosaur bones," she adds.

One of Heidi's favorite hobbies is photographing kids. She also collects vintage photographs of children.

Heidi Chang graduated from the Rhode Island School of Design. She lives in New York City.